For Douglas Vallgren and *Rupert the Dinosaur* – K.N.
For Chloe, to read with her Gran Jan – R.C.

First published 2020 by Macmillan Children's Books
an imprint of Pan Macmillan
The Smithson, 6 Briset Street, London, EC1M 5NR
Associated companies throughout the world
www.panmacmillan.com

ISBN: 978-1-5290-0853-1 (HB)
ISBN: 978-1-5290-0854-8 (PB)
ISBN: 978-1-5290-0858-6 (EB)

Text copyright © Karl Newson 2020
Illustration copyright © Ross Collins 2020

Karl Newson and Ross Collins have asserted their rights to be identified
as the author and illustrator of this work in accordance with the
Copyright, Designs and Patents Act 1988.

9 8 7 6 5 4 3 2 1

A CIP catalogue record for this book is available from the British Library.

Printed in China

# I CAN ROAR LIKE A DINOSAUR

**KARL NEWSON    ROSS COLLINS**

MACMILLAN CHILDREN'S BOOKS

# I can **ROAR!** like a dinosaur.

No you can't.

You're teeny-tiny-titchy-witchy!

You can't scare me.

Oh yes I can . . .

I'm a **DINOSAUR.**

squeak!

# OH NO!

I think I've lost
my Dino-ROAR.
My scary-ness.
My . . . me!

If only I had . . .

**Step 1.** Stand up like a dinosaur.

Put your arms out front, like so.

Now move your head from side to side.

Ready, steady . . .

STOP!

You look like a parsnip! Let's try **Step 2** . . .

Think DINOSAUR.

Wear a toothy
smile, like so.

Arms *out*.
Now . . . shake
your tail!

Ready, steady . . .

Right, **Step 3** – the roar. Arms *out*,
show your teeth, shake your tail – MORE!

Now stomp your feet and here it comes . . .
Ready, steady . . .

RUK
RUK!

CHATTER
CHATTER!

Well, *you* can't **ROAR** like a dinosaur, either!

I could do,
if I wanted to.

It's easy.

Ready, steady . . .

What a silly old bunch!

Don't they know it's rude to stare?

And why did
no one tell me
there's a *chicken*
standing there?!

Now, I must be going.
Time for dinner! Cheeri . . .

OH!

NO!
I'm *not* a dinosaur! That really *was* absurd.
I'm up a tree . . . it's plain to see! *Hah!* I am a . . .

BIRD!